KU-216-329

This book
belongs to

Noah Shrimpton!

This edition published by Parragon Books Ltd in 2014

Parragon Books Ltd
Chartist House
15–17 Trim Street
Bath BA1 1HA, UK
www.parragon.com

Copyright © Parragon Books Ltd 2014

All rights reserved. No part of this publication may be reproduced, stored in a retrieval system or transmitted, in any form or by any means, electronic, mechanical, photocopying, recording or otherwise, without the prior permission of the copyright holder.

ISBN 978-1-4723-5124-1

Printed in China

The BULLY and the Shrimp

Catherine Allison

Kim Geyer

Parragon

Bath • New York • Cologne • Melbourne • Delhi
Hong Kong • Shenzhen • Singapore • Amsterdam

This is Noah Shrimpton.

He lives with his mum and his dad and his dog Dixie.

He's small for his age, but he says:

Being small's not so bad!

He likes dinosaurs and superheroes and drawing in his journal.

He doesn't like carrots. Or stinky socks.

When Noah and his mum and his dad and his dog Dixie moved house,
Noah really didn't like that very much.

He missed his friends and his old den in the garden.

"Starting at a new school's not so bad!" he told himself.

Deep down, though, he knew he was scared.

On the first day, Mum waited with him in the playground.

"They look nice," she said, pointing to a group of children nearby.

"Why don't you go over and say hello?"

But then the school bell went, the children ran inside and it was too late.

Noah said goodbye to his mum and went inside too.

Mrs Johnson, the head teacher, took Noah to find his classroom.

In the corridor, Noah bumped into a very tall boy.

"What's your name?" asked the boy. He was wearing a T-shirt with a dinosaur on it.

"Noah Shrimpton," said Noah with a big, friendly, I'm-new-but-nice smile.

SHRIMP-BOY!

said the boy.

FURTHER INFORMATION

Who are the victims of bullying?

Bullying can happen to anyone at any time. It doesn't happen because a child is weak or at fault.

What can you do if you're being bullied?

- You may find it very difficult to tell anyone what's happening, but telling someone – a parent, teacher or friend – is the first step to making it stop. Getting a sympathetic response is a great comfort, and a bully is more likely to give up if you have someone on your side.

- Try to speak up for yourself, unless you think you are in danger physically, in which case tell an adult immediately.

- Walking away is a perfectly good way of dealing with a bully. It's nothing to be ashamed of. You don't have to listen to his or her abuse. And sometimes, standing up to a bully puts you in more danger.

- Keeping a journal can be helpful: it's a safe, private place where you can work through difficult feelings. It also forms a record of the bullying 'events' that can be shared with others if necessary.

- The important thing to remember is that it's not your fault.

Developed in conjunction with educational consultants: Sandra Hall, Special Educational Needs specialist, and Mary Ann Dudko, consultant on classroom issues and concerns.

What can you do if your child is being bullied?

Carers should look out for the signs of being bullied in their children, such as unusual mood swings, a sudden reluctance to go to school or an inability to eat or sleep.

If a child tells a carer that they are being bullied, the carer should explain that it is not the child's fault and that they are very brave to come forward. Then the carer must address the matter. Depending on their relationship to the bully, the carer could approach the bully directly, or the bully's parents. Often, a serious talk from an adult will be enough to stop a bully's bad behaviour. If the bullying is happening at school, the bullied child's class teacher should be informed.

The child must see that action is being taken in order to believe that the bullying will stop.